Tales of The Other Side

By Nim Barnes

 New Generation Publishing

CHAPTER 1

To some extent there is a fine line between a daydream and a minor psychic experience, especially in early childhood, but as you become older, the psychic experiences become more obvious, perhaps one should say more powerful. I think the clarity of what is occurring becomes more so. Sometimes one can see a person so clearly, it is not obvious it is a ghost, - at least until they suddenly vanish. Occasionally one hears a voice so clearly – just as clearly as a person in the room.

Possibly to help others to realise it is not hallucinations or 'mental illness' I have decide to write some of mine down. Possibly it will be published and people who have had similar experiences will be interested. Possibly it will just be kept for the family and future generations – those who have similar experiences – may think it is worth reading. At this stage, who knows?

The first experience was in 1934. I can remember this very vividly, is being in what used to be called a 'Mail cart', a sort of (now old fashioned) sit up pram, you sat in facing forward – another more pompous version of the present day push chair. I was sitting in mine in the hall waiting for my Nanny to get herself ready to push me out. I think I must have been about 4 years old.

Beside the mail cart I saw a little boy – who arrived with a great feeling of glee and giggly excitement – putting his fingers to his lips to show me I had to keep quiet- and said, very audibly to me,

"I am coming for a walk with you!" He and I both thought it terribly funny. I think I was about 4 and he was about 6, and we felt very conspiratorial!

He wore a green coat, with a dark green velvet collar, and green velvet pot hat – the sort of standard 'Hyde Park gear' of the day, and as we walked along he held the side of the Mailcart and the expedition felt great fun.

After a little while he skipped ahead, put his fingers to

his lips again, so I did not tell, waved and grinned and slowly faded away.

At the time I did not wonder about it. It just seemed like a hilarious experience, but one I should not tell the grown-ups about. So until today I have never told anyone! I wonder if it was his birthday? He didn't tell me this.

Many years later I was told my mother had had a stillborn baby boy two years before I was born. Then I knew who he was.

But later on, during the World War II years, I was in South Wales, where we had gone to escape the bombing. I used to bicycle to and fro about two miles to where I shared a governess. I used to think of him, and often experienced the feeling of joyful camaraderie, although I did not see him the totally clear way I had in the first experience. But I used to talk to him and 'feel' the answers, as I did.

We used to also walk on the mountain, the Cathedine and have 'day-dream' conversations on many, many occasions.

In the winter evenings, my mother, who was not fond of children, used to sit and read in the drawing-room. The rattling of the dice disturbed her, so I was sent to play Ludo with myself in the dining room. This could have been a rather 'off-putting' experience as it was a very large room, and there was no electric light at the time, so I only had one candle to bring with me. The light did not reach the edge of the room, so one was in a small pool of light at one end of the dining room table, with one's Ludo board, counters and dice!

I suppose it is the instinct of all young animals to wonder what is in the darkness. I had also heard some alarming ghost stories from other old houses. I remember the first time, setting up, feeling terribly 'creepy'.

Then suddenly the atmosphere changed completely. It was as though the darkness itself said to me, "No, don't worry, were all here, we'll play Ludo with you. Don't worry about a thing!"

Many, many evenings I went in and mentally said, "Well are you all here?" And the atmosphere of fun and company arrived within seconds. I thought of them all as having their own colour counters, and, although I had to throw the dice for them, and move the counters round the board, it always felt as though there were four of us playing!

Many people may feel this was nothing but imagination, but I know I was too great a coward to have managed it by myself!

I thought of them all as having their own colour counters, and although I had to throw the dice for them, and move the counters round the board, it always felt as though there were 4 of us playing!

CHAPTER 2

When I was a child we lived in Beck Row – or at least week ended there from the flat in London. Before the war I slept in a cottage in the garden with Nanny, and school holidays with Guy, so did not enter Beck House itself very often. I think even then, the old end of it had a rather earie feel, but I can't remember that much about it, from those days.

When we returned after World War II was over, I was (15 years at the time) and I had to sleep in the old end, up the old staircase, which wound up from a door at one end of the dining room. (This part of the house was 1400's. The 'new end' was 1700 and had its own more modern staircase.)

The first time I entered the room, I was aware of a feeling of resentment and hostility. Not a feeling of violence, just bitter, "This is my room, what are you doing here?"

For a few weekends I went into the room as little as possible. I went up to bed with a somewhat sinking feeling. The coldness and loathing of the vibe seemed to intensify.

After a few weekends I walked in one Friday night, and the room felt like a death cell. I sat down on the bed and said, "I can't see you, and I don't know exactly who you are, but I know you are here. I'm sorry I have to turn up every weekend, but I can't do anything about it. We have to share this room. You will have it all to yourself midweek. I am bound to be here at weekends. There is nothing we can do about it. Can't we be friends?"

There was a distant feeling of 'difficult-to-describe'. I knew she had heard me. We were communicating in a sort of way. She wasn't very giving, but the atmosphere seemed to relax a little, if grudgingly.

After that every time I went into the room I would speak to her – either out loud or in my head.

When I arrived on a Friday I would say, "Hello, had a good week?" And I always realised she loved the garden, and would say something like, "Have you seen the roses, aren't they doing well?"

Gradually our relationship seemed to move on a bit. The room became less frightening, and she seemed to grudgingly accept me, or at least to realise that my arrival was inevitable but only temporary and not my fault!

One Sunday morning about 7am the church bells were ringing for the early service – the church being just across the road.

I opened my eyes, and saw her standing by the window, looking out at the church. A little grey figure, a very old lady, grey hair, dressed in black or grey with a shawl. The minute I saw her she faded. Over the years this happened a number of times, but each time I only saw her for a second.

I had a great feeling that she was longing to go to church, but for some reason could not. This wistfulness was poignant. Had she been in love with the priest, I wondered, but I never dare ask that.

Our family owned the house until 1951, when circumstances changed, and it was sold to a local solicitor. The day before we moved out, an American air-force plane from Mildenhall crashed on the front lawn just yards away from the 'old' end of the house. Sadly, the pilot was killed.

I have always wondered, but will never know, if the Grey lady was in any way involved? Had the house been destroyed, of course, it would still have been there in spirit for her, and she would not have had to share the bedroom with anybody else!

Life went on for many years, I really did not think often of her again. One night some time about 1970, when we were at Woodhurst, I woke up and saw her standing at the end of the bed. "You must come", she said, "The walnut tree has been struck by lightning, and they are going to chop it down and destroy it. You must stop that".

5

"I can't come" I told her, "The house does not belong to us anymore". (The interchange with ghosts is not as cumbersome with words as one communicating with each other. The emotions say to all.) She was furious, and she felt I was being useless, and I did not care. She departed and left a lot of quite threatening anger behind her. Perhaps I should have rung up, but I did not. However, I offered a prayer, that if the tree could recover itself, could it be allowed to stay?

Some years later I was in the area. The walnut tree had been a huge and beautiful tree on the lawn beside the house, and luckily visible from the road. I stopped and looked over the gate.

Yes, about three-quarters of it must have been destroyed, but a remnant of the trunk and lower branches were still there, and the branches were putting forward some new growth. She had won, I sent her my congratulations and drove on.

CHAPTER 3

When Peter and I were first married our home was a very nice flat, Clevedon Mansions, near to Sloane Square.

Luckily most of the time we had living-in-help, so I was not alone there terribly often. However, whenever I was, very heavy footsteps used to come down the passage, and, (thank God) stop just outside the bedroom door. One night when the footsteps stopped, my cupboard door flew open. Alarming!

On several occasions, girls we had to help us, who were baby-sitting alone while we went out to dinner, greeted us at the door when we returned, terrified. They told us about the footsteps, and we commiserated.

In due course we learned that the previous tenant (who had lived a rather eventful life in Kenya, before coming to the flat) also heard the footsteps. He used to scream for his manservant who slept in the next room and say, "He's coming to get me".

Unfortunately, it seems the ghost did not realise there had been a change of ownership when he moved out, and we moved in!

When our life there came to an end I was very happy to leave.

CHAPTER 4

When our baby daughter was 4 months old she was given her immunisation by injection into the sole of her right heel. I cannot now remember whether it was the smallpox one, or the DPT. At the time we were told it was a new idea, to prevent her having a scar on her upper arm. At the time we had no idea of all the different things in the injection- mercury, aluminium, calf's lymph, monkey kidney, sheep's red blood cells, chick embryo fluid and fluids from mice and guinea-pigs.

None of this had reached the public domain and at that time our belief that doctors knew what they were doing was absolute.

The partial paralysis started slowly at the age of 8 months. We made no connection with the injection at that stage. The bewilderment and the agony were heart-breaking, made worse by our then doctor's refusal to accept that there was a problem.

Our sanity was only saved by her older brother and she being so beloved, and such a wonderful enchanting and jolly pair of little people to be living with!

The tumours on her spinal cord which was causing the paralysis was not discussed by Great Ormond Street specialists until she was 19 months old. Then it was a mixture of shock and relief for us. Complete horror that a child of her age could have a tumour, and the thankful news that, if it was removed, her paralysis problem might lessen.

I went into Great Ormond Street to be with her, but this meant leaving her poor little brother who was only 3 at the time. For all of us it was quite bad.

The operation was completed with lots of prayers on all sides, and it was not until she had to go back for another check, a few months later, and it seemed that the symptoms were getting worse again, that I felt at breaking point.

The afternoon we were going to an appointment with her surgeon at Great Ormond Street Hospital, I had dressed her up in her best clothes to make it seem like an 'occasion' that she would enjoy. I went into my room to change, and leave, and had such feelings of tears and grief; I put my face against the cold window pane to stop the tears from coming. I could not cry in front of her, as she thought we were going out for a 'treat' – to see Mr Till, whom she liked very much, and I had to make it seem fun.

I was praying and trying to get myself together, when I was aware of a tall white figure standing beside me.

"It will be worse for you, but better for her, there is more to come, but she will live" The voice was audible and the feeling of peace and calm and certainty was all pervading.

The sight of him faded, but the feeling stayed with me for the rest of the day. I had a feeling he did not leave my side, and was able to create the feeling of total peace for the rest of the day.

Another tumour was found, and in due course we were back in hospital and it was removed, but all through the procedure, and the subsequent radiotherapy, I could remember and feel the certainty of the words "she will live".

She did. Thank God. Thank Brother Bernard.

About 7 years later, when we were living at Woodhurst and Trixie Allingham had come to lunch with us, she said to me "There is a white monk standing beside you, he is very tall".

I felt very joyful, but I thought inside my own head, not out loud, "Maybe he is very tall, or maybe he is standing above the ground as it used to be higher". (All of which is quicker to think than to say). Trixie then said "He is laughing and saying no, I am quite tall, although when I am out of doors it is easier to walk where the ground used to be – about 10inches higher than it is now".

I was amazed he had read my thoughts without me saying a word, and also I felt surprised he spoke such 'modern sounding' English, knowing he was from many years ago. (This also passes through your mind very quickly).

Trixie said "He is laughing again, and says 'If I spoke the language of my own time it wold be not understandable in the modern world, - but she and I communicate through thought, so usually words are not necessary'".

All of this was intriguing to Trixie as well as to me. Several times we communicated when Trixie visited and at times I have prayed for his help in moments of crises, but after the very first time I never 'saw' him again.

However, when my most psychic daily help was living in the cottage, (as well as on occasion seeing Ian) she asked me one day, "Did this house use to be a Monastery?"

"No"

"Was there one on this land, before this one was built?"

"No, I don't think so, why?"

"I sometimes see a monk dressed in white. He walks about here sometimes"

"Oh I am so glad; do tell me when you next see him"

"Do you know who he is?"

So I explained to her, the whole story. Her youngest daughter, then aged about 4, was also very gifted, and used to say to her now and again, "Mum, the man in the white dressing-gown is over there on the lawn".

Once, much later on when Rosie was about 9 years, one of our Labradors was in season. She was supposedly in the kitchen, but, being a very feisty lady she had managed to jump out of a window (that I had thought was much too high for her, but where there's a will there's a way!).

The last thing I wanted was another litter of puppies at that juncture, so I called the children and we all went out in our woods looking for her, whistling and calling as hard as we could.

As I set out on my path I prayed and asked Brother Bernard if he could help us find her.

10

Rosie came back with her after a little while and all was well.

"Where was she?" I asked.

"Mum it was really funny, I was going down the lower path at the back of the swimming pool, and I saw what I thought was a very tall man in a long white dressing gown. He was walking about a foot above the ground and when I saw that I thought 'Oh my God it's a ghost'. And, when I did he turned around and gave me such a smile, I did not feel frightened of him at all. And he pointed down the path towards the wood, and he sort of put it in my head 'she's down there' and then he just disappeared. He seemed so terribly nice, I wasn't frightened of him, so I just ran down the path and there she was. It was lovely. Now here she is!"

And there she was – not pregnant. Thank God for Brother Bernard.

CHAPTER 5

1961 until 1970 we had a little house close to the sea in Middleton-on-Sea. Before we bought it we were in a furnished let down there for the summer holidays. We walked past this house every day on our way to the beach. We saw the For Sale board that was in the front garden. It was seductive, and after a week or two we got the estate agent to show us over.

It was 'fully furnished' to the extent that the table was still laid, and a half empty ketchup bottle was on the table! It was not occupied at the time, so we felt a bit as though we were trespassing!

We had a redoubtable local lady helping us with our cleaning and laundry, and I went back and we chatted about the visit.

"It was the house of a very good friend of mine. She ran it as an 'old people's home'. Just three old ladies. She looked after them very well. It was a very happy place. She had been a hospital matron in her day. A lovely lady she was.

"They wanted to hold a Women's Institute meeting there, and they wanted some of the chairs bought downstairs, and she would always be one to help. She carried a heavy chair down the stairs, they shouldn't have let her. They should have helped her. A lot of young ones were there, arranging things, they could have done better. But at the bottom of the stairs she had a heart attack, and they helped her into a chair in the main room and she died. Very quickly. But there was a huge panic, they called the ambulance, but it was too late. Then they called off the meeting, and the old ladies had to be collected by their relatives. They were all whisked away. I suppose they were given a meal before they went. Sounds as though it's time someone went into the house and gave it a spring-clean. Sounds as though it had better be me. I don't mind it. I knew them all they were great friends of mine.

12

"Are you going to buy it? If so I 'll go over this afternoon!"

We bought it.

Our children grew up with this as their holiday home. Our second son was born in a local maternity hospital one summer, and came back there when he was 5 days old.

There was the beach and riding, the seafront in Bognor and the band in Hotham Park in those days when the tide was in. We had a lot of very happy summers, Easter holidays, and half terms there. It was one of my favourite places.

Eventually, life seemed to have come to the time to move on. I went down for one last day to tidy up the garden for the last time. I felt terribly sad to be saying goodbye, and kept putting off shutting the front door for the last time, knowing I then had to give the keys in to the agent, and that was the last time I would be there.

I stood in the hall, close to tears, and said, "I have to say goodbye".

A voice quite close to me said, "Would you like to see a picture of me?" It was an older woman's voice, and I recognised that it would be Mrs Halsey's friend who used to live there. I realised she must have felt very much as I felt then, having been carried away so suddenly while her three dependants were still living there.

I said "Yes" rather wondering how on earth this could happen.

"The back of the airing cupboard" I was told. I was amazed. It was a huge airing cupboard, but we had used it for nine years, and never found anything in it except the used towels, bed-linen and our aired clothes etc.

I went upstairs and opened the doors, I could see nothing.

"Right at the back" said the voice.

I wondered if they had been there while she was alive, but had been taken out when she left. I was not sure what size or shape I was looking for. I kept groping around.

Suddenly I felt something behind the hot water tank.

13

Like a package of some sort. I pulled it out. In it were 5 photographs. Herself as a very young girl, herself in hospital uniform, herself as an older woman.

I sat on the stairs and looked at them. I felt I was meeting her. I told her how pleased I was to do this.

In some way, in a way I cannot explain, it made leaving Kestel a bit easier. I took the photos home and Peter and I looked at them and thought what a strong good-looking woman she had been, and how Kestel still held some of her spirit.

I know she had a nephew to whom the house had been left, as we had bought it from him. I contacted him via the agent, who still had a record of his address, and sent him the photos.

He was very pleased to have them.

CHAPTER 6

Although my two older children have never appeared to be psychic in any way, my younger son appeared to be even more receptive than I was, from a very tiny age.

By the time he was born we had moved to another home, a smallish London house, 21 Ormond Gate. He was conceived there.

I remember carrying him up and down the bedroom, held up to my shoulder, to shush him off to sleep, when he must have been about 3-4 months old, and seeing he was smiling into the semi-darkness with a really brilliant smile. I wondered at the time if he saw somebody. I did not, so about that particular incident we will never know.

However, at about 18 months old he would often smile and wave at 'somebody' and as his speech developed, he would say "lo man" (hello man) and then turn to me and say "see - man".

One day he jumped off my knee and ran forward saying ""'Lo man" Then turned around and looked at me with a face of complete astonishment and said, "Man gone – 'eres' man gone?"

I said "Man gone, man will come back another day"

Mentally I said to the man, "Don't disappear again like that, it frightens him. Go out of the door before you levitate".

From that day onwards 'he' always came through an open door, and obviously used to wave goodbye to Tosh, when he went. Tosh used to wave and say "Bye bye man" Then the 'man' went out through the door. Tosh would run and look for him, then come back and say "Gone".

Tosh slept in our bedroom there, when he was about 2years old, as he still liked a '10 o'clock feed', I would bring him up a bottle, prop him up on pillows and let him feed himself while I got ready for bed.

Quite often he would look around the room and say, "Allo man", put the bottle back in his mouth and suck on.

Sometimes he would say to me – "Look man". In due course, he would pull the bottle out of his mouth, wave it cheerily and say "Bye-bye man".

The spirit was one of huge kindness and clearly a love of small children. I never felt at all alarmed. I did feel rather intrigued. To this day I will never know who it was. Tosh cannot remember the incidents at all.

The house had been inhabited by a large Indian family prior to us. I wonder if there was an elderly grandfather who enjoyed babies and that had perhaps died there. I still have no idea if that is the case. From the atmosphere it was a very kind and loving soul who made the house happier. One of my happiest experiences.

CHAPTER 7

It was in 1965 that my husband and I bought a new house in Surrey. By that time we had our three children and our youngest son had just turned 3 years.

I should have been more aware of his 'psychic' powers at that stage, but as, during the experiences in London he was not able to talk very much, I had rather forgotten about this.

We had been there a few weeks I think, when during the night he appeared at our bedside and said "There's a man in my room and he keeps throwing black stuff over me". "It's a bad dream", I said. "Come into bed with me and Daddy". He climbed in between us and went to sleep.

The house had been altered quite a lot when we bought it, and there had been a fireplace in his bedroom, which had been blocked up. His room was now arranged, his bedhead was in the place the fireplace had been. As he was very small at the time, and the rebuilding had taken a long time to do, he had never seen it in its original state.

The next few weeks, the 'dream' occurred several times, and I asked him more about it. He was very matter-of-fact. "My dream-man walks about in his pyjamas. He picks up a bucket and goes downstairs and comes back with it full of black stuff, and throws it all over me. So now I get into your bed before he gets back".

"I see", I said. "I think we have put your bed in the wrong place. That used to be a fireplace".

He cheered up immediately. "So he's throwing it on the fire?"

"I think so; I think it must be coal".

"It isn't lumps, its black stuff"

"Maybe coal dust"

"Yes, I think so".

"So if we move your bed, things will be better". We went upstairs.

"Yes, put it over here. He walks in through that wall, if

17

the bed is here, he will walk through the end, but that's alright 'cos my feets don't go down that far".

Gradually it became clear that his 'dream-man' had known the house very well before it had been altered. It had not surprised me that he had walked through the wall into Tosh's bedroom, as the wall had not been there prior to our arrival. The bedroom had been 19foot long, and we had pinched five foot (plus a few feet from the next room) to make Peter's dressing room.

Our 'dream-man's' bed, would have been in the five foot that was now missing!

At a psychic level, Tosh and he positively communicated for some time, it was obvious it was quite interesting to Tosh at that time, small though he was, that the house had been different.

"At night", he told me, "It is all different downstairs".

"Tell me about it", I said.

"Well", he said. "There's a passage through to the back bit". Pause. "There's another door in the hall".

"Where does that go to"?

"The study".

"I see".

"Then you go down the passage so you are into the kitchen place".

"I see".

"Then you can go out the back and there are two sheds".

"What are they for"?

"Coal and wood".

"Are you sure"?

"Yes, that's where my dream-man goes".

The description was 100% accurate of how the house had been previously. This was a purely psychic discovery as Tosh had never followed his dream-man downstairs.

On another occasion.

"At night there is a door here". (Pointing to a place in the hall wall.)

"Yes, there was one, but we closed it up".

"Did you? How did you do that?"

"Well we got a builder to do it for us, we took a wall down, and so the passage came into the room, so we only needed one door".

"Did you? So where did the study go?"

"Well the old study was a part of the room where the television is now".

"So it's gone away?"

"Well sort of, yes. We altered things a bit".

"My dream-man used to do arithmetic in there".

"Did he? What is arithmetic?"

"Oh, I don't know. He did it".

Another time he said to me.

"My dream-man is standing at the edge of the drive. He is dressed all in white, even his shoeses is white". He thought this was very funny.

I said "Perhaps he is going to play tennis".

"Yes, he has a tennis racket in his hand".

Later I learned that the main lawn had been a tennis court. I hope he was joined by three other players.

I thought I needed to know more about our 'dream-man'. "Is he young?" I asked.

In those days, all the young men were wearing their hair very long, and only my husband's generation had 'short back and sides'.

"Well" was the reply, 'He has a Daddy's haircut, but I don't think he is a Daddy".

I learned then that it was interpreted that a proper haircut was taken as a sign you had achieved paternity!

"So he has hair like Daddy's but he looks very young?"

"He has the flattest hair you ever did see. Sort of shiney."

Some years later, when I knew who it was and I saw his photograph, I saw a lovely Brylcream image. At the time I did not know so much.

A short time after this, I decided to try to find a psychic lady who might be able to tell me more. I contacted Trixie Allingham, through the College of Psychical Research.

She was a wonderful character and brilliant psychic.

She arrived at our house, and within minutes said, "I hear a voice, a young man saying sorry about the ashes. Are you keen cricket fans?"

"No, but I think I know what he is talking about, I have asked him not to throw coal on his bedroom fire in the night."

"Have you? Does he do that then?"

I told her all about our history. She said, "I will tell him not to disturb the little boy."

We spent quite a long time communicating with him. I learned he had been killed in the war, and had really loved Woodhurst where he had grown up. He was very sad to leave Woodhurst, where he deeply wanted to spend the rest of his life. Trixie introduced him to some other spirits to help him to move on, but I told him how much we appreciated the wonderful atmosphere he made, and said to visit Woodhurst at any time he wished. He told me, through Trixie, how much he loved the garden and the woods, and I promised to communicate with him whenever there was a really beautiful vista – and I did.

Some years later I had a daily help who was far more psychic than I was.

On the first occasion they met, she said to me. "There's a young man in the drive looking at the daffodils".

Just shortly before I had communicated with Ian and said. "The daffodils are really lovely, do come and see them." I felt elated; I felt I really did get through.

Later in the year, when I had thought of him, and told him how beautiful the garden was in the snow, Sue said to me, "Your young man's on the back lawn in the snow, looking at the trees."

Time and time again, I would communicate with him, without Sue knowing this, and time and time again, she would confirm with me that he had arrived.

On one occasion, I had a great friend coming to convalesce after an operation, and Sue and I were in the spare bedroom making up the bed. My friend had lost her brother in the war. Sue looked out of the window and said. "Your young man's on the lawn talking to another young man. Very tall with fair hair". I knew who it was.

Later talking to a friend who lived locally, and had for many years, and known the previous owners of the house, I learned that his name was Ian; he had been killed in World War II, coming up through Italy. I think he had been in the Scots Guards. I never 'saw' him. I only felt his presence. When he arrived I used to feel an icy wind around my ankles. Then we used to talk.

Years later, we were all in Church on Christmas Day. I was intrigued to see a large black butterfly flying around the Church. The Church was decorated and I thought it must have arrived from foreign parts or lived in a local greenhouse. He came and settled on the pew in front. He also settled on Ian's memorial plaque on the wall. As we sang Christmas hymns, he seemed to fly around the church, settle on the newels, and on the font, but not in agitated way – just floating around very happily.

As we came out of the Church, I said. "Wasn't that amazing, that huge black butterfly?"

"What butterfly?" asked my daughter.

"Don't say you didn't see it? How could you not see it? It settled on the pew several times".

"No Mum, you're imagining it".

"I can't believe that you didn't see it".

"There was nothing there Mum. You were imagining it"

"Yes there was", said our youngest (then aged about 5 years). "I think it was the dream-man wishing us a happy Christmas".

"Rubbish how could he turn into a butterfly"?

"I don't know but I think he knows".

"That's utter rubbish".

Well maybe. Maybe not. I believed him anyway.

CHAPTER 8

When moving into Woodhurst we had a considerable amount of work done on the house, and I became great friends with the architect's wife. She also had quite a psychic side to her – and in many cases a more robust approach to any problems it involved than I had!

The house they lived in was often haunted by a previous owner, and Susan would frequently tell me that she had seen her, and told her to "B....r off". I felt a bit sorry for the ghost actually, as I never felt her presence and did not think she was aggressive. She had been an elderly lady who had gone into a local care home for some years before her death, and probably just regretted leaving the house.

Twice Susan had a premonition of a plane crash from the local aerodrome of Dunsfold. In those days, this was a place for test-flying new planes. The second time she told the people who ran the aerodrome, and they were very friendly, and appeared interested and grateful, but the crash happened anyway. Five people were killed, two in the plane and a family in a car it crashed into.

The third time she told me she had an uneasy feeling again, I suggested she contact them again and she did, inviting them round to drinks, and was able to tell them she felt there would be a disaster again quite soon, although it was hard to give an exact date and time. They left having had quite a jolly evening, and she felt there was nothing more she could do.

The next Saturday I took my youngest son over to Runfold for a friend's birthday party, and having dropped him off I was going home down a country road, when I started to shake and shake and feel I could not control the car. I parked at the side of the road, and shortly felt as if I was falling and falling from a great height. As I was sitting still on the seat of my car, I had no idea what was happening. It went on for some seconds, and then I had an enormous sharp pain in my back, like a tremendous hard blow, other pains in my limbs, but I felt very glad the feeling had stopped, and nothing much worse had happened. I sat for quite some time recovering, under the beech trees, and eventually drove home, still somewhat shaken, and also anxious, or had this been to do with the premonition Susan had had? Had there been a disaster?

I rang her and told her. She was a strong personality and somewhat dictatorial. "No, nothing has happened. I can't think what all that was about. Did you have too much to drink at lunchtime?"

"No, and anyway this happened long after that."

"Well I think you're fussing too much, and I would forget it!"

The next evening I got a phone call, with quite a lot of laughing.

"Sorry about yesterday, you were right, the crash happened this afternoon!"

"Was the pilot killed?"

"No, he came down into an oak tree. His broke his back, but they got him down. He is in hospital, but will survive. I suspect you know that?"

"Well no, the whole thing left me really after the blow in the back. I could not tell what was happening, it all seemed to end".

"Yes, well he passed out. Then the ambulance people got there and gave him painkillers that knocked him out to get him down from the tree. You did well darling, I should have rung them up and told them".

"Wouldn't it have been too late? Didn't it happen while I was going through it?"

"No, no darling, you just had a premonition. It didn't happen until this afternoon. They've only just got him into hospital. The plane's a right-off, of course. Tell me if you have one of these again, and I'll ring them".

"I did tell you".

"Yes, well next time I will take it in".

"Good".

There never was a next time- luckily.

CHAPTER 9

When my youngest son was 6 years old, we had the unfortunate experience of our two boisterous Labrador puppies pushing him backwards into the cold frame. A huge shard of glass went into his insides. It was a terrifying moment, but we went into Mount Alvernia and he had an operation to check the damage. Luckily the internal damage was not as bad as it could have been. We spent about 6 days in Mount Alvernia in the same room and all went well and he came out fully mended.

On about my fourth night in there, there was huge frost.

Tosh was fast asleep in the bed next to mine, when, in his sleep, he suddenly sat bolt upright and said very loudly, "The water is pouring down the stairs, GET ANDREW, GET ANDREW".

He then flopped back, and went straight back to sleep. In the morning he did not know this had happened.

I lay in the darkness and puzzled about what to do. If it was happening at home, there were 5 of them there, so presumably they would know, and could get help if needed. If it were at Andrew's own house, he must surely know and be able to do something. I could not think where else it was happening or what to do, so eventually I went to sleep again.

The next morning quite early I rang home. And was told, "No, nothing's happened here, Mum, we are all fine. I expect you just had a bad dream".

No I knew I did not.

I rang my architect's home and spoke to his wife. (He was the Andrew I was meant to tell in the night.) Had anything happened? No, he had no emergency calls, and their own plumbing was perfect. "One of you has a very vivid imagination – not sure which one". I was told.

I was completely non-plussed, and somewhat frustrated.

A couple of days later, when I got home, I called a great friend of mine, who lived across the lane from the little house where Andrew had lived with his first wife, who had since passed over. This was something I was not aware of, as I had not known him at the time.

"How are you?" I asked.

"Totally exhausted" was the reply. "I have had the most ghastly two days".

"Oh my God, have you? Whatever has happened?"

"Well a couple of mornings ago, water kept pouring down the drive, and we could not think where from. Then we traced it back to Overhill Cottage, where it was pouring out from under the door. The house is empty, so I had to collect the keys from the agent. Then Elizabeth and I went in in wellington boots. It was pouring down the stairs. It was inches deep in the hall. By the time we had got in, it had been pouring down for hours. The hall and all the downstairs rooms were full of water. You have never seen such a mess. We have spent the last two days, trying to clear things up and get things dry…. It has been a nightmare."

"Well how did you and Tosh get on in Mount Alvernia, is he alright? That's the main thing?"

"Yes, thank goodness, they found he was not as damaged as we had feared, so they stitched up the main wound, and he has mended well. BUT the strange thing is…." And I told her the story.

"Two nights ago?"

"Yes, wasn't it strange"?

It was then I learned this was where Andrew and his first wife had lived, long ago.

"Oh, so this is why the message was, 'Get Andrew".

"Yes, I imagine so, but they might have told you the address. It could have helped a lot. How did they expect you to know where it was happening?"

"Maybe next time I should ask?"

"If it happens again, dear, do. A little more detail would be very helpful. But I think she could have thought of that herself".

"I suppose they could not activate Tosh for more than a

few seconds".

"If she had said just said Overhill Cottage, you could have rung me early next morning, and we could have gone in straight away. There would not have been so much mess. No, I think I shall tell them they have not done too well. Mark you; she was not a very efficient lady when she was alive".

Not a very successful experience!

CHAPTER 10

After moving to Woodhurst I met a great friend locally, an amazing, kind, sympathetic and very sweet person, and we did quite a lot together.

She had had two marriages that had sadly broken up, but not, I feel due to faults on her side. She was feeling very vulnerable and had lived through some very heart-breaking situations.

Tragically, while we were away on holiday in Switzerland, there was one event too many, that tipped the balance.

It was her younger son's 21st birthday and she yearned to see him. There was a present for him. She rang him and asked to see him, where she lived in Surrey was very close to the former family home. He told her he was going to London and did not have the time.

She went to her flat in London, and rang him from there and asked him to come in. Sadly he said, "I am going to the theatre, I will come and see you tomorrow."

The visit to the theatre being with his father, step-mother and girl-friend, this was just too much.

She took her own life, alone in her flat that evening. She just felt alone, left out, rejected. She felt she no longer had her own son. It was a moment that should have passed, as she had many friends, but at that moment she was alone, and she took her own life.

We only heard this a couple of days later on our return to England.

I had felt uneasy about her while we were away, and tried to ring her on our return. There was no answer, I hoped it meant she was out with friends, but still felt uncertain.

Later I heard the news from another great mutual friend. I felt devastated. It was evening and I wandered out into the rose garden. I could not think what to do. The pink roses were very beautiful and this seemed to soften the moment. I prayed "God give her roses. Masses of roses. It may help. Give her a huge field of pink roses – as far as she can see, give her roses."

Then I said to Paul, (my brother who is on the other side) "See if you can help her. I don't know where she is. I think she is feeling devastated, but I don't know where. See if you can find her. See if you can help her."

I went indoors. I had to get supper ready. Life had to go on.

A few days later I saw old Trixie. I told her the news of the death, but no more. I was not sure what had happened.

"Yes dear, she did take her life. Not a very sensible thing to do. Afterwards she was alone in her flat for several days. They were devastated when they found her of course. Her elder son and a woman friend of his. They couldn't get into the flat. They had to break the door down. Yes, they got the police to do it.

"Yes, her spirit was still inside and still stayed there after they were gone."

"Ask her what happened. I think she has been feeling a little better, I have felt it, am I right?"

"She says she wandered around the flat for two days, then the break-in and she did not know what to do, then in the evening she found herself wandering in a huge field of roses. Pink roses. It lifted her heart a little, it was very beautiful. Then she heard a man's voice, very, very softly calling, "Yvonne". Calling very gently, from quite a way away at first. Gently coming nearer, he kept calling, then waving and she felt much happier, he came through the roses and was talking to her.

"It all sounds better, doesn't it dear. I think she will be looked after. I wouldn't worry too much anymore".

I missed her sorely, but I did not worry so much anymore.

CHAPTER 11

Sometime while my elder son was at Stanbridge Earls, it was decided by the school that they should be given 'useful projects' to occupy their time during the summer holidays. One of the tasks the school was given was to help return the garden of a rather derelict old house, which was much in need of care and attention.

It seemed to me not such a brilliant idea at the time, as the house was hugely in need of repair, and although I think the idea was that it should be offered for sale, it looked an unlikely winner. The left hand edge of the property was flanked by a high wall, about 4 or 5 yards from the house. Behind this was the railway line, and an alarming number of noisy trains went by at regular intervals.

He was meant to go down every day for a couple of weeks, and there was a young caretaker/gardener to direct the operation.

Each time I dropped him off I had a great feeling of deep depression emanating from the surroundings. Where the trains came crashing by, it seemed to make it even worse, although it was not at all clear why.

The caretaker, who had been there for a few months, trying to put a lot of things right, was looking for a new position. He found it all very depressing.

The last time I took Jonathan there I was waiting on the path in front of the house, and I bent down to tweak a few more weeds out of the beds at the side of the path. I was surprised to feel a great feeling of peace and serenity as I did this.

All the odd emotions connected to the building were so puzzling; I could not really work out where it was all coming from.

I rang Magda. It wasn't too far from where she lived.

"Do you know ....House?"

"Yes, I do, but I think it is empty, isn't it? It hasn't

30

been lived in for many years".

"Yes, but I have been spending a little time there, taking Jont, these holidays. It's very strange place – it's so gloomy. I can never wait to get away."

"Yes it would be. They put a railway line in right next to it. The owner was so driven mad by the noise of the trains going by, especially at night, he couldn't bear it. It had been his family's house for generations. He spent years writing to the railway companies, and asking them to stop the night trains. They never did of course, so the family could never sleep. One evening he went out with his gun into the field behind the house and shot himself. The whole situation and the lack of sleep had driven him mad.

"The police were called in and they thought he had fallen over, climbing a style and it was an accident, but his poor wife knew what had happened. She was so grief-stricken. She moved away – I don't think they have ever managed to sell the house."

"I am sure you are right about what happened. This is why the place is so agonisingly depressing".

"Yes, it always has been. At one time the local vicar asked some nuns to come and help in the front garden and to pray for the occupants. I think for a while it seemed a bit better. They were a very sweet and kind group, and they prayed for absolution – but the house has never sold. Goodness knows what's going to happen to it".

I don't know what happened. Now, writing this, I feel I should have done more. But I have to admit, I didn't.

CHAPTER 12

Many years later when Tosh was about 16 years and was at Hurstpierpoint, he was home for a weekend.

"Mum", he said. "Can you come and sit with me downstairs".

"Yes, OK".

"Do you remember my Dream-Man, many years ago?"

"Yes, I talk to him quite often".

"Yes, well. At Hurstpierpoint we were trying a Ouija Board Session, to try to talk to the people in the hereafter – well you know what happens, you have a glass upside down and it takes off and goes from letter to letter and spells things out. Have you ever done it?"

"No, but I've heard of it. A lot of people think that the people around the table are pushing the glass around, but I really would not know. So what happened?"

"Well his name is Ian, isn't it? Well the glass really took off and took itself about the table. We couldn't have stopped it. It said. "This is Ian. Don't do any more. It can be dangerous. I will see you at home if you want to see me". Then it stopped".

"I think it was probably good advice. You could get the wrong spirits coming to you. So do you want to see him again?"

"I don't know really, I haven't actually seen him since I was about 5. Now it feels a bit creepy, really".

"Well I'll tell him that. Don't do any more Ouja Board; you don't know what will happen. Leave it all for the moment. When you become older you may become quite psychic. Who can tell?"

Writing this now, about 30 years later, so far he has not, and maybe those on the other side would like to be left in peace. Who can tell?

In years to come, shall we develop the mobile phone further than it is today, so we can contact them? Do they want this?

CHAPTER 13

One of my fascinating meetings with Trixie was a day I was with her with a few other people, and she suggested we all tried to extend our 'psychic readings' ie experiences. So we all spent a little time seeing what we could 'come up with'.

I saw an old fashioned kitchen, with a dresser and old kitchen table in the middle and something very agitating happening at the other side!

There was a huge old-fashioned stove, with a fire inside it, but surprisingly a fire going on above it. Under the ceiling, not apparently anything to do with the fire, but a huge blaze about nine feet long, just fire and smoke. As I watched it, it crashed onto the top of the stove and into the hearth, setting fire to the mat.

I described it as above to Trixie.

"Oh yes, dear, that did happen. A spark from the stove must have blown upwards and started it – a whole Yorkshire airier full of towels drying caught fire. Luckily I walked into the room just in time. Yes, they were all blazing away – and then the ropes burnt through, and the fire just fell – onto the stove and the rug. Yes, I had to call my sister and we both ran around and poured jugs of water on it. Terrible it was, we were both terrified. But we got it out. But SUCH A MESS. Water and black burned material and the wooden bars were all burned. And if we hadn't found it when we did the whole house would have been burnt to the ground. It was terrible."

"How long ago did it happen?"

"Oh we were children, I was 14, and my sister was 12, so many years ago".

At the time Trixie was in her sixties, so it had been some time ago. But I described the kitchen to her, and yes, she said it was the room. One of her most vivid memories, and impossible to pluck out of the air, and see it all happening again!

CHAPTER 14

My experiences at the Old Vicarage were traumatic and horrendous. But knowing that the person who created them has now repented and has forgiven I feel it would be unfair and possibly unwise to go into it all.

I have decided not to. To be honest, I suppose I am also a bit of a coward, and want to 'let sleeping dogs lie'.

There is only one incident, that was from a different era, and I have to admit two of the experiences were not mine.

Sue Savoury, who had worked for me at Woodhurst for some years, but had had to leave due to family problems of her own, came back to help our move into the Old Vicarage. She had been helping in the garden, and came in for coffee.

"I've just seen the little girl on the side lawn".

"Really what is she doing here?"

"She is playing with a hoop. I think she passed over some years ago".

"Really? Oh I see. A spirit?"

Sue was more psychic than I ever was, and she could also communicate more successfully with those in the next world.

"She was wearing those sort of long pants they used to wear, with frills around the ankles. I could not think what they were, so I asked her". She said, "Nankeens".

"Really? You were able to talk to her?"

"Yes, she was a friendly little soul".

Later in the year I was sitting on a bench at the far end of the lawn, with a friend of mine who was a doctor. She suddenly said to me "Who is that child?"

"What child?"

"The one playing over there".

I couldn't see her, but I did not want to upset anyone, so I just said, "Oh I think she lives around here".

"Well why is she playing in your garden?"

"It doesn't matter, I don't mind".

"Why is she wearing such strange clothes? Is she going to a fancy dress party?"

"I expect so".

"Why don't you ask her?"

She looked back up the lawn. "She's not there anymore, where did she go?"

"Maybe she went to her party. Not to worry".

"But how did she get out of the garden? Is there a gate down there?"

No, was the short answer, so I supposed that I had to break it to her.

"I think it was a little spirit person who does play on the lawn at intervals. I have never seen her, actually, but I would expect you to be psychic. Because you are Scottish – Gaelic and they usually are quite psychic. Do you see ghosts often?"

"But didn't you see her just now?"

"No, but she has been seen twice before by Sue when she has been weeding the garden for me. She seems very friendly; I would not worry about it".

"So she is a ghost, but you do not worry about it?"

"Well no, I don't worry about it, unless their intentions are aggressive, and she certainly is not".

The doctor was slightly unnerved however, and left shortly afterwards.

At another time I did see a man and woman, walking around the garden, clinging to each other, and both consumed by grief. The sight was agony. I was so sad for them.

I feel sure they were her parents, who loved her so much, and had to cope with the unbearable moment of her death. It must have been just a memory that manifested, as by now, they would have passed over too and so would be re-united with her.

I expect, even now, it is hard for them to forget the agony of that day, and perhaps those terrible moments recur to them even now.

There is a gravestone in the churchyard that records the death of a little girl aged 9 years, in that era.

CHAPTER 15

The village of Witley has many, many ghosts; in fact it is quite hard to hear of a house that is not haunted by them, as indeed are the church and the pub!

In the church there is a thin, elderly, slightly round shouldered priest in a black habit with dark hair and eyes, who is overcome with anger and grief.

Before the time of Henry VIII the church would have been Roman Catholic, and the feelings convey that he was full of disgust and rage that his church and his parishioners were being taken from him. There was also some fear that he might be killed.

The parish story, that I was told, was that he left for Suffolk one night, to try to get help. Whether he was killed in Suffolk, or whether he returned to Witley and met his end there, I am not sure. I have a feeling he hid for some time – somewhere, filled with anger and grief. I think he returned to Witley at some stage, but it may have been after his death. He has been seen many times in the Church, during the service, and on other occasions.

The little stone cottage next to the Church is said to be alarmingly haunted. In the eight years we were in the village there it seemed to change hands three or four times. I did not learn who that ghost was, but I suspect it may have been the priest.

The pub 'The White Horse' was said to be haunted by a lady in Victorian clothes, who sat in the alcove seat by the fire. She was thought to be Lady Hamilton waiting for Nelson. Tragically it is believed to be the night he did not return.

I never saw her, but many people have.

The manor house and at least three other houses are all said to be haunted, but I have not got the full stories for them,

One of the cottages near to the Old Vicarage though was said to have a ghost, who talked. The old lady who lived there said they talked to each other quite often.

Going round with the Flag Day charity box – something I often did in those days, - I rang the doorbell and waited. The old lady was obviously out.

Then a voice just behind me said, "Hallooo Nim!" I looked round, but could see no-one. I started to leave down the path when a voice said "Don't goo Nim". I looked again. There was nobody there. I regret to tell you I left at some speed!

CHAPTER 16

My other great friend Magda who was very psychic was Czechoslovakian but her family had moved over to England just before the war. Her husband was an art dealer, and she was a wonderful artist with a huge talent. She did a lot of portrait painting, and had an uncanny knack for getting the personality of the sitter on the canvas.

She lived in Haslemere. We knew each other very well for years, and had several occasions when we communicated our psychic experiences. Her parents-in-law had passed on some years before, but they too had lived near Haslemere. She told me she was often aware of the presence of her mother-in-law, of whom, contrary to usual comedian's tradition, she was extremely fond! "Let me know if you see her", she said.

These experiences come to you, like a dream, and you see and feel things at the same time. Others, who do this, will know what I am talking about, those who do not will be sceptical!

I saw this very elegant lady get out of a little old-fashioned car in Magda's drive. Very neat 1920's hair style, dark red hair, and a little fox terrier jumped out with her. She was dressed smartly and neatly in 1920's style in a very pretty silvery-grey dress and jacket. She took a few steps towards the house and then faded.

When I told Magda, she said "I think that was my Mother-in-law's. She had a little fox terrier".

She showed me her mother-in-laws picture. It had been kept in the drawer in her husband's desk, and so I had not seen it before. Yes, it was her.

Another time, to my great surprise, I saw a very old-fashioned bath, full to the brim of dark red roses. Such an amazing sight, I could not think why this could be. When I went to see Magda I told her about it.

"Yes" she said, unsurprised. "They used to do that.

When they were giving a huge garden party, they used to order all the flowers early in the morning. The servants had a downstairs bathroom, and they used to put them all in the servant's bath for a good soak before she arranged them".

"A whole bath full?"

"Well you saw them, didn't you, so you know better than I do! – But yes, they used to give the most enormous parties – and she used to do the flowers all morning, Bill says".

On another occasion I saw her riding through Haslemere on a tall horse, wearing some sort of cream and crimson fancy dress. The horse was a tall chestnut one, with a lot of presence. They both looked very together and very dignified. I told Magda. "Yes, she used to ride in the local pageants. Dressed in Elizabethan costume". I am told.

I think that must be what I had seen.

CHAPTER 17

Another story Magda told me about her mother-in-law was that the birth of her first two children, who were twins, a boy and a girl, had been very hard to bear. The girl had arrived, and the doctor had packed his little bag and was departing. Her mother-in-law was suffering more extreme contractions, and the doctor came back from the door to tell her these were just 'after pains'.

She then had another massive contraction and almost immediately Bill was born, rather to everybody's consternation at the time! The outcome left her very exhausted and anxious.

The second pregnancy was viewed with an alarming dread of the whole birth process, at least at the outset. However, I was told, she had such a sweet and sympathetic nurse-midwife for the whole time, that this birth went well, and she felt enormously joyful and restored to health when Audrey was born.

I saw a long picture of the scene a day or so after the birth the mother very weak and tired but very happy, and deeply grateful to the nurse looking after her, with whom she had formed a deep bond. I saw them talking together, and very early in the morning the nurse pushing her out in a chaise-longue onto a logia or patio, where there were a lot of flowers, and it was full of early morning sunshine, and a huge feeling of peace and serenity.

The baby was brought to her, and she turned to the nurse and said, "I have found a name for her – Aurelia - it means the dawn". They were both delighted.

I feel the father's view was that this should be 'corrected' to Audrey as a compromise! I am sure he felt Aurelia would be too 'showy' and so objected, and this was a disappointment to her. But he may have been backed by other relatives, and so his decision prevailed.

But I think the moment on the logia, where the sun was on the flowers, and her baby was bringing her so much happiness and recovery of strength – that was a moment she would always remember. Moments of told joy are rare but this was one of them – therefore possible to tune in to, and in a way, share with her.

Although this must have taken place about 35 years before I felt it, and that experience was 40 years ago, to when I am writing now, it is still a magical moment, and I am so glad to have been able to share it.

CHAPTER 18

Sadly, however, the next moment I picked up on another occasion more of tragedy, but an acceptance of this, as all resistance had left her.

I saw her walking through a garden with a feeling of deep sadness. Looking at all her plants and vistas as though, in her heart of hearts, she felt this was the last time she would see them. At the end of the walk, she lent on a stone parapet overlooking an ornamental pond, which was full of beautiful water-lilies.

I felt very deeply that she thought she was looking at them for the last time. That she loved them and that this was a sad occasion, but that this was just a hint of the total feeling of sadness. The feeling of agonising dread went much deeper, but there was an acceptance that it was inevitable.

I rang Magda and told her. I felt it was much worse than if it was resulting from their selling the house – moving away – her being left by her husband or anything else I could think of.

I knew when you communicated with the spirit world you can raise questions in your mind to ask what you are seeing/feeling, and they can be answered by the feelings you are experiencing and tell you whether they are the truth or not.

Magda told me the sad true story.

After the birth of the three babies, which took place in her late 30's, she was given to feeling tired, and needing to rest at times during the day. She was what they used to term in those days 'not strong'. Her husband became disappointed and impatient. He wanted her to give parties, go riding, play tennis, go on holidays and generally 'do things'. Part of the time she found it too exhausting.

He consulted the local doctor, and between them they decided that a hysterectomy would be the answer. It was an operation that had been fairly recently introduced to the doctor's armoury. It could give women some freedom from the depressing limitations of being feminine!

Magda's mother-in-law was horrified. Surgery was new and dangerous in those days (1920's) and not to be undertaken lightly. However, the doctor was very confident it would answer and solve all the problems, and the husband was delighted.

Tragically, she must have known the outcome in advance. This is what I was picking up. The twins were only 14 years and Audrey was 11 years. She could not bear the thought she could be taken from them. Somehow she must have known what the outcome was likely to be. But she could no longer resist the male pressure.

Tragically, she died under the anaesthetic. Without the operation she might have lived until old age.

The afternoon of the water-lilies, she must have been very much aware of what could happen.

CHAPTER 19

Magda was a fabulous artist. Talented and very much in touch with her sitters, this made their personalities stand out in the paintings.

She rang me one morning.

"I'm painting a portrait".

"Good, who of?"

"Actually, I'm not going to tell you, I'm wondering if you might pick up some stuff about her".

"Maybe. Can I know a little more about her?"

"No, I will be intrigued to see what you can tell me".

"She is not sitting for you, so you can ask her?"

"No".

"So she has passed on?"

"Yes".

"A long time ago?"

"Yes".

"So how are you going to know what she looks like?"

"I have studied quite a few previous portraits, and they are not all very good. I think I can do better!"

"So you are seeing her psychically, I suppose?"

"Yes".

"Tell me…"

"No, I don't want to tell you anything. This may confuse you. Tell me what you pick up".

"OK, if I can".

"You will".

A couple of days later I rang her.

"Hello, I have picked up something, I think, although there is no way of checking what is true or not, without any history".

"Keep going".

"I think she went abroad somewhere as a young girl – about 10 – 11 years old – I'm not sure. She only had two dresses to take, a red one and sort of toffee coloured one. As she had to be smart she was sorting through a lot of bits of ribbon and lace and embroidery. Apparently the intention was to unpick things and sew new little bits on to make them look like new dresses all the time. I think there was a pair of new sleeves for one of them! There was mixture of ecstacy and panic.

There was also a dear little brown dog, who so much wanted to go with her, but she was going to have to be left behind. Very sad parting".

"I have been picking up the history a bit. Somewhere, she was walking down a long path in an avenue of trees. She was meeting with the man she actually loved, but was never going to be able to marry. This is where I picked her up, and felt I should paint her".

"Are you going to tell me who it is we are talking about?"

"No".

A while later.

"I think I have picked up the lady who is your sitter again".

"Tell me".

"I am picking up that she was killed deliberately and yet, it doesn't seem to have been regarded as a criminal act. And I seem to pick up that she knew it was going to happen, but there seems to have been no effort made to avoid it".

"Carry on".

"Well she seems to have been totally well and totally sane, but to have been waiting for death to happen. She seemed to know it was coming. But she seemed to know she was unable to avoid it".

"So did you register that it did?"

"Yes, she seemed to be very close to me. It seemed to be a sudden choking, so horrible she could not take another breath, it felt rather as though her throat had closed up, suddenly, and I said to her, "Oh you could not get enough air?" and at that moment she seemed to be beside me, and said, "Too much air really" and there was a light tinkly little laugh, as though the whole thing was quite

46

funny. It was really weird, but as though she had huge courage, and could cope with her death – in the most unusual way. I still can't make out what quite happened".

"Now I know you were on the right wavelength. Well done, Nim. It was Anne Boleyn. Come over and see the picture".

"Oh my God, I did not pick that up. How tragic it all was".

"Come and see".

It was a very beautiful portrait.

CHAPTER 20

At the time it seemed that both Magda and I were very able to have quite clear psychic experiences without difficulty. Well I suppose at any time, it is never difficult! It either happens or it doesn't. It seems to be more a question of the other side being able to tune in with us, rather than us tuning in with them.

Sometimes my intelligence is rather lacking when it comes to interpreting them, so it is useful to know those closer to the source, to get it right. One day after a visit to Haselmere, where Magda lived, I saw some huge enormous pine woods, full of well-grown dark trees, carpeted with a layer of brownish-grey old pine needles, and for the most part up quite steep slopes, At the time I thought 'Scotland'? But it was quite warm and the ground was dry.

I saw a man with a small boy with him, probably 6 – 7 years old, and they were examining the pines, and the father was explaining to the son, how you found out which was a good strong pine, what the wood was worth, which strength of wood was used for which purpose, and so on. The little boy seemed very interested, and kept asking questions and taking it all in. The language was not English – not even with a hugely Scottish accent, - but when it is a psychic happening you are able to take in what is going on. I thought maybe they were visitors to Scotland, as the language was different, but this vied with the actual feeling that they were very much at home.

They carried a basket, and in due course they sat down, and the little boy got out a white cloth and set it out with some food – I can't remember really what – or even if I knew at the time, - but they sat there, eating and talking, and the dusk gathered, and the stars all came out. They talked about the stars, and which star was what, and then the little boy settled down to sleep on the pine needles.

It all faded, but I felt it was related to Magda, so the

next day I rang her to tell her.

"Yes, it was my mother and her father".

"No, it was a little boy".

"No, it was my mother dressed like a little boy!"

"???"

"When she was born she was the third daughter, and the birth was so difficult the doctor said my grandmother should not have another child. In those days the doctors word was law.

"My grandfather was grief stricken as he was longing for a son. He wept and wept. And then it was decided between them that she would be dressed as a boy, and have her hair cut as a boy, and he called her Bobbichi (little Bobby) in Magyar".

"So this was all in Czechoslovakia not Scotland!"

"Oh it was all in Czechoslovakia. You don't build everything from pine in Scotland. Weren't they speaking Magyar?"

"Yes, but in a general way, you pick up the general gist, no matter what the language. He was teaching her how to test the pines in some way".

"Yes, he had to decide what they were used for. Houses, flooring, pillars, furniture. They needed to vary. He could judge if they were right for the job".

"And he wanted to teach your mother?"

"Yes, and she wanted to learn and be an expert".

"And did she?"

"Only in a limited sort of way. When she got to puberty her mother and sisters said the game had to end. She was developing, her periods were starting, and her breasts were enlarging. I think it was quite a massive turn around moment. A few of the neighbours knew 'he' was really a girl, but not all of them did. It was a very emotional time for the whole family. Especially for my mother, although some people tried to be very kind, and say they had always known. But my grandfather was devastated. It was almost as though he had had a son, and he had died. He became rather morose. It was hard for him. Probably harder than we realise".

"What did your mother feel about it? Does she talk about it?"

"Sometimes. She feels it was a very strange time for her. And she feels it is a shame she only had two daughters. I think a grandson would have meant a lot to him. But I think you have just seen and felt one of his happiest times. I think he was feeling then there would be a miracle of some sort and Bobbichi would grow up as a man".

"What a shame it couldn't have happened".

"Well, hang on, if it had happened I would not be here!"

"Sorry, yes".

"Let's go and have tea with Mummy, and just get her to tell us about it, she can still remember it well."

"Let's do that".

We did and her recollections painted the whole picture. She was a very amazing woman, and her telling the story gave it another perspective. To let life play games with you to that extent and come through it, you have to be very strong and have a sense of humour.

Luckily she was, and she did.

CHAPTER 21

One time when Magda and Trixie were together and having a conversation, Trixie said, "Ann is here to talk to you, and say how happy she is that you are married to Bill, and all is so joyful".

Magda did not know who Ann was, at that stage. She said to Trixie. "Trixie, I can't think who that is".

Trixie then gave Magda the names, Ann, Mary, George, David and John.

Magda could not recall the names as anyone in a group, who she knew, so felt Trixie must be making something up!

She saw me shortly afterwards and told me the names.

I said. "Oh I know a family of five children, all called those names. They are the Blackwells".

Magda said, "Oh Ann Blackwell".

I then heard that Bill had once been engaged to Ann Blackwell, who had tragically had leukaemia, and had died ahead of the wedding. He had been devastated for several years before meeting Magda.

Magda had never known Ann, but it was a very happy message to receive that Ann was thrilled how happy Magda was making Bill.

CHAPTER 22

Magda and I both did automatic writing at that time. I never did small closed up writing, but let my hand do capitals as they came to me.

Sometimes it was not successful, and few words emerged. Sometimes it went ahead quite swiftly, if briefly, and wrote things I needed to read.

Once, quite early on, I wrote the 'message' IVAN CO MALE. I hadn't a clue what it meant. I did not know anyone called Ivan, but something told me it was a message to show to Magda.

Immediately she said. "Yes, it is Ivanco Male, you just left a gap in Ivanco. Ivanco is my cousin, Male means ill. I must ring up and see what is happening".

When she did so she found out Ivanco was very ill, I think it was pneumonia. We both prayed for his recovery, and the illness passed.

The second message was in Slav, a language spoken by servants in Czechoslovakia. Magda having left there so young – seven years old – she could recognise it, but not fully interpret it.

However, the first word she saw 'NIKOLAI' she recognised – "Oh he was our cat."

I had not been sure of the word and wondered if, it referred to a grandparent or friend, so I was quite intrigued to hear that.

Magda then told me that packing up and leaving in such a tremendous hurry and panic, had been a great cause of grief to her and her 5 year old sister as they adored their pet cat, and could not bear the fact that he was being abandoned.

She took the note round to her mother who was able to tell her it was from their old cook, and it was interpreted as:

"Nikolai was all right. I took him home with me. We both lived through the war, and he lived to a very old age".

Magda and her sister were thrilled to hear this – albeit about 30years too late! Such a shame they did not hear it earlier, it would have made them so happy!

The third and final message I had sent to me in Magyar, so Magda herself was able to interpret it herself.

She read it out to me "Pot plants. There are not two anymore. Why?"

I could not see that this made any sense, but Magda was a trifle taken aback.

A very old friend of hers, and her mother, had been terminally ill. Magda took her two pot plants, which remained with her for some weeks, but when she realised she was dying before too long, she asked Magda to take them back and look after them well, as she loved them.

Magda took them home and looked after them until after the death, but then, as she felt the two of them were rather large and taking up too much room, she gave one to a friend.

The message left her feeling rather guilty and wondering what to do.

We were both rather surprised that the person sending the message did not realise exactly what had happened.

She was a slightly ferocious lady and perhaps <u>did</u> know, but was going to think how to put this to Magda in a way to make her feel somewhat chastised.

We both decided to send the message back, that both pot plants were flourishing, and there was no cause for concern. I wondered if we would hear again, but we did not.

CHAPTER 23

I had one other very brief psychic experience with Magda, which made me very anxious, and I told it to her, as I could not quite work out what was going on

Being such a talented and intelligent person, who had been here in England since the age of 7 years her English was absolutely faultless, and it was quite hard to remember she was Czechoslovakian.

I told her one day: "I had such an interesting psychic time last night. Someone was having a huge and impassioned argument – but not in English.

"He was trying to persuade somebody to do something that they were very reluctant to do. But he was sitting behind a large desk on a swivel chair and he swivelled it around to speak around the side of the desk, and kept talking on, with tremendous vigour and emotion.

"The person he was talking to was in a state of indecision. He was determined to get through their reluctance, but it was taking a lot of doing. He was not bullying, but I think helping, but he was very forceful and went on a very long time.

"I felt it may have been something to do with you.

"Do you think you know what it was all about?"

"Yes, it was the local school master in Czechoslovakia. He persuaded my father to evacuate us to England at great speed. The invasion was about to take place. My father was the local doctor so was very reluctant to leave. But the school master was certain he should take my mother, my sister and me run to safety as quickly as possible.

"He arranged the journey and in the end we left within 24 hours.

"My sister and I were 7 and 5 years so we were told we were going on holiday, but it was a very long journey. It was all done in a matter of few days and we ended up in a guest house in Wales."

"Quite a different life really".

"It must be".

"If it hadn't been for the person you have just been seeing, we might never have got here. But he had a hugely forceful personality and persuaded my father, just in time".

"I am so glad he did, or I would never have known you".

The force and emotion of the man's persuasion will always be an experience I remember witnessing.

CHAPTER 24

On the next occasion Magda rang me one evening. She was part-owner of a small antique shop in Petworth, and used to go to London sometimes to buy objects for sale. She had an eye for the perfect item and came down with many beautiful and unusual things.

"I'm in trouble". she said. "I have bought a small wax figure of a boy child. It is rather beautiful, but I believe it is haunted, I have had the most unnerving feelings, and three times on the way down I nearly crashed the car. I am terrified".

"Where is it?"

"I've left it in the car. But it seems to release huge feelings of anger and hatred, quite overwhelming. Not the feelings you would expect from a baby at all. It is so strange".

"Can you take it down to the church?"

"Not now, I could be killed in the lane, its dark now".

"It needs exhorcism; can you get your priest to come?" (Magda was a Roman Catholic).

"I could try".

"Can you find out its history? There must be a reason for this? Who could tell us?"

From much enquiring over the next few weeks the history emerged.

The little boy had been the son of a rich French family – the only son in a family of a lot of girls, and dearly beloved by his father.

The mother had made him pose naked for the wax sculptor, who had taken all day to complete the little figure. The little boy, at the time about two years old, had complained to his mother about being cold.

His nurse had begged for him to be given some clothing, but the sculptor had insisted on carrying on. He was sitting in front of an open fire, and the little figure is sitting with his hands held forward – evidently he had been trying to warm them.

Tragically we were told; he died of pneumonia a few days after the sitting. His father was beside himself with rage and grief. He could not bear to look at the little wax statue. The child's mother on the other hand, felt she could not bear to part with the little figure.

In his fury, the father wanted the figure destroyed, (I think he may also have felt like killing his wife, as she had allowed this to happen.) They called in their local priest, we were told, and he had suggested that the figure was given to a local convent, where the nuns could pray for the soul of the little boy.

The mother was agonised that this figure of her beloved little boy was to be taken away, but the priest (and the father, I think) felt this was the best possible solution that could happen.

When Magda told me, I saw the funeral. A huge French church, grey and white interior, the priest in black, a kind authoratative man, able to take charge, but very well aware of the grief of the mother and the uncontrollable rage of the father.

The statue was blessed. A small white cloth was placed over the genitals, and the nuns accepted the gift. I am aware they prayed for the baby. I am sure it helped him. I don't think they had the strength to pray for the father – or perhaps by that time he had gone beyond helping.

Both Magda and I prayed they had found each other, and managed to feel and understand each other's grief. We felt the situation had been eased.

The priest took the little figure home with him; I think it had been released by all the reconciliation of the family on the other side. There was a feeling that the hatred had subsided. I think the father of the figure could only be helped by meeting his son. I hope this happened.

Yes, it did

Lightning Source UK Ltd.
Milton Keynes UK
UKOW02f1320021116
286691UK00003B/17/P